CANDYBYTE

Diana Foronda

13HORROR.COM BOOKS
An imprint of
DIZZY EMU PUBLISHING
1714 N McCadden Place, Hollywood, Los Angeles 90028
dizzyemupublishing.com

CandyByte
Diana Foronda

First published in the United States
in 2022 by 13Horror.com Books

CANDYBYTE

Diana Foronda

<u>CANDYBYTE</u>

INT. LIVING ROOM - NIGHT

A hand turns on the TV. BILLIE, a late 20-year-old woman,
lives alone inside of her cleaned apartment. She eats a Fuji
apple while watching "The Late Night Show with Jessie."

On the TV screen, JESSE, a non-binary, late 20 year old,
waves to their audience and goes to their desk.

                    JESSIE
          Hey, y'all! Welcome to "the Late
          Night Show." Tonight we have a
          special guest, and she is the
          designer of Robotech's newest
          creation, Candy. Can we get an
          image for our audience to see?

An image pops up showing an apple-shaped smart home with the
words: "Candy your smart home friend until the end."

                    JESSIE (CONT'D)
          Isn't she gorgeous? This cis-woman
          here tonight is one of the top tech
          influencers, and my personal hero.
          Please welcome to the stage,
          Charlie McMann!

Everyone in the audience applause CHARLIE, a late 30-year-old
ginger-haired woman, as she enters the stage. She waves to
the crowd and shakes hands with Jessie. Then, she sits down
on a chair next to Jessie's desk.

INT. STUDIO - NIGHT

                    JESSIE
          Hello Charlie, thanks for stopping
          by.

                    CHARLIE
          Thank you for having me.

                    JESSIE
          Tell us, how did you create Candy?
          How did you get started?

Charlie smiles.

                    CHARLIE
          When I was an intern at Robotech,
          my assignments were organizing
          files, sitting at the front desk,
          working on spreadsheets, and taking
          out the trash.

                    JESSIE
          Ah, those were the internship days,
          taking out the trash and cleaning
          up the kitchen.

The audience laughs.

                    CHARLIE
          While I was on my trash duty, I
          found some mysterious old rough
          drawings of an apple smart home
          design. I began studying the
          drawings.

In the audience, MONICA, a late 30-year-old Charlie's
assistant, sitting in the crowd looking at Charlie with her
lips closed and slowly smiles.

                    CHARLIE (CONT'D)
          I researched statistics and reviews
          of other smart homes, and I thought
          to myself: "Why can't we have a
          creative, smart home? There are
          enough smart homes out there that
          have a square or a circle shape,
          but why not have a smart home that
          is shaped like an apple?"

Audience murmurs and nods.

                    CHARLIE (CONT'D)
          You see, having an apple as a smart
          home is sweet. It's never bitter,
          but the catch is, you don't eat
          that type of apple. Candy is filled
          with all metal and wires in the
          machine. So let's not bring Candy
          to these wild food challenges you
          see on the internet.

                    JESSIE
          Like the Cinnamon Challenge?

                    CHARLIE
          Yeah, like the Cinnamon Challenge.
          She doesn't taste like Fuji, Cameo,
          or Evercrisp.

                    JESSIE
          You heard it here, folx! Candy is
          meant to be your friend, not food.

                    CHARLIE
          It's 100% not edible.

Charlie and Jessie laughs.

> JESSIE
> So Charlie, wanna bring out Candy?

> CHARLIE
> Sure!

Audience applause. Jessie's staff rolls in a table covered in a red blanket. The two staff leaves, and both Jessie and Charlie walk towards the covered table.

> JESSIE
> Alright Charlie, are you ready?

> CHARLIE
> Yes.

> JESSIE
> Okay, y'all count down: 3, 2, 1!

Charlie pulls out the red blanket off the table and reveals a shiny metal apple shaped like smart home remaining still on the table.

The audience ah-ing and oh-ing and applauding.

> JESSIE (CONT'D)
> Damn, she's pretty! So what can Candy do, unlike any other smart homes?

> CHARLIE
> She can help you out with directions when you're on the road, she plays your music playlist from your phone, her batteries last long, and you can talk to Candy. You can talk to her about personal issues, fashion advice, and much more.

> JESSIE
> Okay, okay, so Candy is just like your average A.I. friend. I like that. Let's talk to her!

Charlie turns to Candy.

> CHARLIE
> (To Candy)
> Hey Candy!

Candy lights up.

INT. LIVING ROOM - NIGHT

On the TV screen, the crowd ah's and oh's on the look of the bright delicate apple. Then, finally, Billie stops eating her fruit.

On the TV screen, Candy remains in a bright glowing look when she's on. Candy speaks in a high-pitched tone similar to Jennifer Tilly.

                    CANDY
               (On TV)
          Yes, Charlie?

                    CHARLIE
               (On TV)
          Do you like this outfit?

                    CANDY
               (On TV)
          You look great, Charlie! However, I
          recommend changing your necklace
          into a simple look. Try to use
          pearls or a sapphire necklace, not
          just some stone rock necklace.

INT. STUDIO - NIGHT

                    JESSIE
          Oh, is she referring to your
          detailed bronze ruby necklace on
          your neck?

Charlie turns to Jessie and holds up the Heart of Damballa on her neck.

                    CHARLIE
          Yes, she is.
               (To Candy)
          Oh Candy, you know I just got this
          necklace from the street market in
          Queens. I want to support the
          community there.

                    JESSIE
          That's right, support your local
          businesses! It's a pretty necklace
          you got there, Charlie. It has a
          good apple theme to it. Ruby
          necklace, red blouse, red lips -
          all apple like!

                    CHARLIE
          Thank you, at least someone
          understands.

                    CANDY
          Oh ha, funny. You know, you're the
          worst, why did I ever agree to be
          on here?

                    CHARLIE
          Okay, goodbye, Candy.

Candy shuts off. Audience laughs.

                    JESSIE
          Give Candy some love, y'all!

The audience and Jessie applause. Jessie laughs.

                    JESSIE (CONT'D)
          So you told me backstage that
          anyone can buy Candy now online,
          correct?

                    CHARLIE
          Yes, Candy is available for pre-
          order. It's 30% off from its
          original price. You can go
          to robotech.com and search for
          Candy.

                    JESSIE
          A-maz-ing! Y'all better get your
          smart home now at robotech.com! The
          website will appear below on our
          screen for all who want to check it
          out.

Jessie turns to Charlie.

                    JESSIE (CONT'D)
          We're about to wrap it up. Thank
          you, Charlie, thank you, Candy!
          This is Jessie signing off!

Both Jessie and Charlie wave at the camera.

INT. LIVING ROOM - NIGHT

Billie grabs her TV remote and turns off her TV screen. She
opens her laptop and types in Robotech at the search page.

On Robotech's website, it says, "Candy! Your ultimate go-to smart home and your best friend."

Billie reads the reviews, the detailed specs, and the description of the apple-shaped smart home. Then, she grabs her wallet and clicks the "buy now" button.

INT. SUV - NIGHT

Charlie closes the door, and the driver drives.

                    CHARLIE
          Monica, isn't this great? The
          audience loved us!

                    MONICA
          Oh, Charlie, they loved you and
          Candy being there! It's all
          wonderful! I overheard positive
          feedback from the audience after
          the show. Things are looking up!

                    CHARLIE
          Good, I'm glad to hear that.

Charlie texts constantly on her phone.

Monica pause.

                    MONICA
          Out of curiosity, what's your next
          plan?

Charlie remains texting.

                    CHARLIE
          One second.

Charlie stops texting and puts down her phone. She sighs.

                    CHARLIE (CONT'D)
          Honestly, I don't know what my next
          plan is.

Charlie looks out the window and pause.

                    CHARLIE (CONT'D)
          I think Candy could use a 2.0 look,
          but I would love to see how this
          original Candy will sell.

Monica nods.

                    MONICA
          Yeah, remember when we were
          interning for Robotech back in
          2006? You told me you had an
          invention idea, but you decided to
          shift gears to design Candy
          instead?

                    CHARLIE
          Yeah, I remembered that! The micro
          earpiece invention.

                    MONICA
          What happened to it?

                    CHARLIE
          That concept wasn't my passion. It
          was something I found through a
          film long ago. I wasn't entirely
          into designing it or look deep into
          it.

                    MONICA
          Oh yeah. If you weren't entirely
          into it, it would have been a
          disaster. Sounds like a terrible
          idea.

Monica pause.

                    MONICA (CONT'D)
          By any chance, did you see the
          latest sale statistics on Candy?

                    CHARLIE
          No, I haven't. Instead, I've been
          avoiding the sales percentage
          tracking feed and hoping for
          positive things rather than the
          negative.

                    MONICA
          There's nothing to be nervous
          about, Charlie. You're
          exaggerating.

Monica takes out her tablet from her purse. She opens the
live feed of the pre-sale of Candy.

                    MONICA (CONT'D)
          Look.

Charlie stares at the tablet from Monica's hands and she
takes the tablet from Monica's hands. She looks at the live
statistics feed of Candy's consumer percentage pre-sale.

                    MONICA (CONT'D)
          We've reached 75% since the late-
          night show.

                    CHARLIE
          Wow, we're almost to the green
          light.

Charlie hands Monica the tablet back.

                    CHARLIE (CONT'D)
          Yeah, you're right. I shouldn't be
          nervous about this smart home.

                    MONICA
          Wanna grab a drink? Just like old
          times?

                    CHARLIE
          Where? Alfred's Bar?

                    MONICA
          Why not?

Monica faces the driver.

                    MONICA (CONT'D)
          Change of plans Riley, we're going
          to Alfred's on 58th street.

Charlie looks out the window of the car.

INT. ALFRED'S BAR - NIGHT

Monica and Charlie walk into Alfred's Bar. They both breathe
in the smell of cocktails and beer. They smile with glee.
They see old cherry wooden tables remain standing just like
from their memories.

As they make their way to the tables, people are dancing the
night away filling with laughs and smiles.

Monica spotted one of the tables that have their names carved
in them. Located in the corner near the bar, labeling: RT
Internship '06.

                    MONICA
          Oh, sweet Alfred's!

                         CHARLIE
               Still hasn't changed a bit. Glad to
               see people are still dancing.

Monica nods.

                         CHARLIE (CONT'D)
               Hey, I'm going to use the bathroom.
               I'll be right back.

                         MONICA
               Wait!

Charlie turns around.

                         MONICA (CONT'D)
               Want an appletini?

                         CHARLIE
               Sure.

Charlie walks to the bathroom, and Monica looks at her menu.

INT. BATHROOM - NIGHT

Charlie gets out of the stall and washes her hands. She looks
at herself in the mirror, staring at her tired face.

She breathes in deeply and slowly exhales out.

She takes a couple of paper towels, and turns off the sink
knob. She throws the paper towels in the trash.

She walks to the door and locks it.

As she remained in the center of the bathroom mirror, she
lightly lifted her Heart of Damballa necklace and holds
tightly while looking at herself in the mirror.

FLASHBACK

EXT. ASTORIA - DAY

At a street fair, Charlie encounters a seller selling
jewelry. All various stones and gems from Arizona to Egypt.

Charlie stares at the Heart of Damballa necklace. The seller
raises the Heart of Damballa necklace in front of her.

                    SELLER
          This necklace will save your life.
          Just say these words: "Oh Damballa
          sateria, Macomb, Shango - give me
          the power to rule the world. Leveau
          mercies du bois chaloitte secoise
          entienne mais pos de morte!" Then
          you wouldn't have any more
          worries.

The seller hands the Heart of Damballa necklace to Charlie
and she studies it.

FLASHBACK ENDS

INT. BATHROOM - NIGHT

Charlie stares at the necklace.

                    CHARLIE
          Oh, Damballa sateria, Macomb,
          Shango - give me the power to rule
          the world. Leveau mercies du bois
          chaloitte secoise entienne mais pos
          de morte!

Charlie looks at herself in the mirror.

                    CHARLIE (CONT'D)
          Wishing I was Candy to rule the
          world and face my fears.

She hears the door rattles, and someone knocks on the door.

                    WOMAN (O.S.)
              (Drunk)
          Hurry up, I gotta pee.

Charlie turns to the door.

                    CHARLIE
          Shut up!

INT. ALFRED'S BAR - NIGHT

Charlie walks to the table where Monica sits, and Candy is
placed between the two bloody red delicious appletinis. The
appletini drinks are filled with little apple slices of
Macintosh on top of the salted rim around the martini glass.

A server comes to their table and hand them five tequila
shots.

                    SERVER
          Welcome back guys, it's on the
          house!

Both Charlie and Monica thanked the server as they leave.
Charlie sits down and raises her shot glass. She stares at
Candy on the table.

                    CHARLIE
          To Candy!

The two clink and drink their shot glass.

INT. DANCE FLOOR - ALFRED'S BAR - NIGHT

Many shots later, Charlie and Monica both dancing with
everyone on the dance floor. Monica holds Candy and dances
with it while drinks her appletini. Charlie chugs her drink.

Then suddenly, Charlie feels dizzy and confused. Her eyes
circling around her vision.

Charlie coughs up blood on her hand and faints down to the
hard wooden floor; SMASH! Her head bleeds out. She starts
feeling nauseous.

Charlie coughs up and vomits blood on the floor. She gasps
for air until her neck lays back and her veins violently pop
up of red and blue from her chin to her chest.

Monica runs and sees Charlie on the bloody floor. She drops
Candy and screams.

Charlie remains paralyzed.

Charlie's eyes locked to her bloody hand with a broken
appletini glass. Through her imagination, she sees herself
holding Candy from her bloody palm hand.

The necklace shines as Charlie coughs one final time. A white
spirit comes out of her mouth.

Charlie's shell closes her eyes.

EXT. ALFRED'S BAR - NIGHT

Charlie's spirit drifts away as she screams.

EXT. ROBOTECH HQ - NIGHT

In the windy night, Charlie's spirit lands inside the
building.

INT. ROBOTECH OFFICE - NIGHT

At the development room, multiple Candy smart homes are being
shipped out. Charlie's spirit intertwines into a tornado and
leads her trapped into one of the shipping boxes which labels
Billie's apartment address.

INT. LIVING ROOM - DAY

Billie opens the door, carrying her mail with a small box
from Robotech. She puts the rest of her mail down on her
island table and opens the box.

She turns on her TV while gathering materials from the
Robotech's box containing the smart home, the charger, and
the user manual.

Billie sees the TV news anchor discussing the weather for
this week's forecast. Billie mutes the TV.

Billie reads the instruction and downloads the Candy app on
her phone. She plugs in the charger, but the charger color
remained green as she raised her eyebrows and unplugs the
charger.

                    BILLIE
          Hmm, guess they charge it in
          advance?

Billie turns to Candy and speaks.

                    BILLIE (CONT'D)
          Hey Candy?

Candy (aka Charlie) wakes up and speaks in a mimic tone of
the original voice of Candy.

                    CANDY
          Hi, I'm Candy. What's your name?

                    BILLIE
          Billie.

Candy scans Billie and her entire apartment. First, Billie
looks over the manual of scanning. Then, she swiftly reads
the instructions of how Candy will be connected by simply
scanning who you are.

                    CANDY
          Billie, nice to meet you. I love
          your apartment!

Billie flips pages for Candy's commands.

                    BILLIE
          Candy, please play indie music?

Candy plays calm, soothing indie music from Billie's
playlist.

INT. LIVING ROOM - DAY

While the indie music continues to play, Billie sits down on
her couch and continues reading the Candy manual.

On muted, the TV news anchor discuss the latest headlines of
Candy featuring Charlie's death and her autopsy report of
alcohol poisoning.

                    CANDY
              (Transitions back to
               Charlie's voice)
          Are you kidding me?

Billie gasps. She looks up and sees nothing in her living
room but looks at her smart home in the kitchen. She walks to
the kitchen.

INT. KITCHEN - DAY

Billie looks at the knife from the dry rack from the sink.

                    CANDY
          They still haven't found my
          murderer yet?

Billie quickly grabs the knife and holds it outwardly to
Candy.

                    BILLIE
          The fuck, you talk?!

Candy quickly turns around and faces Billie.

Billie's apartment lights flickering on and off.

                    CANDY
          Billie, I wouldn't do that if I
          were you.

Billie drops her knife.

Flickering stops.

                    BILLIE
          Okay, okay, I'm sorry.

She quickly takes out her cell phone and dials 9-1-1. Then,
out of the blue, her phone dies.

Billie calmingly breaths.

                    CANDY
          You better help me find my murderer
          before they get away with another
          kill.

Billie overlooks the living couch with the TV featuring a
photograph of Charlie. Billie looks at Candy.

                    BILLIE
          You're her.

                    CANDY
          Guilty.

INT. KITCHEN - NIGHT

At the table, Billie eats a sandwich while looking at Candy.

                    CANDY
          I don't know why I'm stuck here.
          First, I was drunk and partied at
          Alfred's, and the next thing - I'm
          dead, and I'm inside of Candy!

Candy sighs.

Billie grabs her laptop and types in Robotech on her search
engine.

                    BILLIE
          What did you do before you were on
          that TV show?

                    CANDY
          I went to the street market in
          Queens and bought a necklace.

                    BILLIE
          It looked like the Heart of
          Damballa necklace.

                    CANDY
          You know the necklace?

                    BILLIE
          My grandmother was into witchcraft.
          She told me about the curse on that
          necklace. Your soul is alive, but
          you will likely to remain in the
          smart home forever.

                    CANDY
          Shit! All the seller told me is to
          say some encourage words and hold
          the necklace tightly.

Billie searches the Heart of Damballa and find the spell on
her laptop.

Billie shows Candy her laptop that highlights the spell
similar to the one the seller encourages Charlie to say.

                    BILLIE
          You just created a spell to keep
          you alive, did you know that?

                    CANDY
          Great, just great.

                    BILLIE
          Look, it's not easy to get out of
          the smart home. You may need to
          find the murderer who made you dead
          and attack them. And once they're
          dead, you will be out of your shell
          and into your spirit form.

Candy pause and she sighs.

                    CANDY
          Think you could help me out?

                    BILLIE
          Only if you help me find your
          murderer, I can't do this alone.

                    CANDY
          Deal.

INT. MR. CURTIS' OFFICE - DAY - 3 MONTHS LATER

A knock on the door.

                    LEE (O.S.)
          Come in.

Monica opens the door.

                    LEE (O.S.) (CONT'D)
          Ah, Monica! Thanks for coming. Have
          a seat.

MR. LEE CURTIS, a 60-year-old CEO businessman of Robotech
with a British accent, remains sitting on his chair.

                    LEE (CONT'D)
          Now, I'll make this quick.

Monica sits across from his desk.

Lee pause.

                    LEE (CONT'D)
          Monica, it's only been a couple of
          months since we're thinking about
          Charlie and her passing. Her legacy
          will always be with us, especially
          with her project on Candy. And you
          know, we have to start thinking
          about a new concept in honor of her
          legacy. So I thought you'd be
          perfect for taking over as the Head
          of Design at Robotech.

Monica widens her eyes.

                    MONICA
          Me, why?

                    LEE
          Well, you've interned with us
          before, and you have been close to
          Charlie. You know our products, our
          mission, and our purpose to provide
          our consumers with the best
          technology out there. I think you
          would bring great content to our
          company. What do you say?

Lee extends his hand.

Monica spreads her lips across her face wide. She shakes his
hand.

                    MONICA
          It would be an honor, sir!

INT. CHARLIE'S APARTMENT - DAY

Billie enters Charlie's apartment. She sees Charlie's mail collection on the floor, her messy drawers, her laptop around her cluttered desk, and her polished closet filled with blazers and long sleeved button shirts.

Billie takes Candy out of her backpack and holds it in the palm of her hand. Candy turns around in a 360 degree, scanning her apartment.

                    CANDY
          Yeah, sorry for my crap lying
          around. My internship binder should
          be near my laptop.

Billie goes to Charlie's desk.

                    BILLIE
          Jesus, at least you could have
          warned me about your place.

Billie sees a 2" black binder that reads, "Robotech Internship 2006."

                    BILLIE (CONT'D)
          Is this the binder you want?

                    CANDY
          Yes!

Billie flips through the binder, which contains Charlie's notes on her internship responsibilities and her notes on Candy.

On a few pages over, there's a group photo of the interns. Billie sees Charlie, in the middle, smiling on the image and sees Monica across the bottom left of the photograph.

Charlie's front door is being unlocked. Billie quickly grabs the binder, her backpack, and Candy while running to the nearest closet in the hallway.

Through the blinded doors, Billie sees Charlie's family, her mom, her step-dad, and her siblings opening the front door.

Charlie's family carries a few brown boxes and heads straight to her bedroom, closing the door.

                    BILLIE
               (Whispers)
          Who are they?

                    CANDY
               (Whispers)
          My family. They never supported me
          after I got my internship, but I
          can't believe they came all the way
          from Michigan.

                    BILLIE
               (Whispers)
          What was it like growing up?

                    CANDY
               (Whispers)
          I didn't have a lot of friends
          growing up. My family was the only
          thing I relied on. But they were
          too busy to support me. My mother's
          a smoker, and my siblings moved to
          different states, my step-dad and I
          got in touch from time to time, but
          the last time I reached out to him
          was after graduating college.

                    BILLIE
               (Whispers)
          Seems like the care now that
          they're here.

                    CANDY
               (Whispers)
          Bullshit. For my mother, she wants
          something out of me. I know it's
          about money. I remembered she
          always asking me for money to pay
          the bills, but mostly I know she's
          using my money to buy weed all the
          time.

Billie pause.

                    CANDY (CONT'D)
               (Whispers)
          Let's get out of here.

Billie quietly opens the closet door and leaves.

INT. BILLIE'S APARTMENT - LIVING ROOM - NIGHT

Billie looks at Candy.

                    CANDY
          I'm glad I took the opportunity to
          intern at Robotech, or I would have
          stayed home and looked for a job or
          gone to grad school in a different
          state. Worst case, I could have
          worked at a fast-food restaurant in
          my hometown.

                    BILLIE
          How did you create Candy?

FLASHBACK

INT. ROBOTECH HQ - DAY

YOUNG CHARLIE, 21, takes out the trash in each different
desk. She goes one by one to clean up the trash while people
are working.

                    CANDY (V.O.)
          While I was interning at Robotech,
          one of my responsibilities was to
          take out the trash.

Charlie sees a crumbled piece of paper with a unique design.
She take sit out of the trash.

                    CANDY (V.O.)
          In one of those cans, I spotted an
          old design draft. Someone may
          think, "this draft is garbage; I
          got a better concept than this." So
          I took that piece of that old draft
          and made it my own.

Charlie goes to her intern desk and start designing in her
sketch book. She rips the old design of her micro earpiece
project and designs Candy in a new piece of paper.

                    CANDY (V.O.) (CONT'D)
          At the end of Robotech's internship
          program, we created a PowerPoint
          presentation to develop a new item,
          like smart home or anything, to
          develop new technologies for our
          consumers. My original idea was an
          A.I. micro earpiece that could be
          useful for anyone who wants a new
          friend. I was writing other ideas,
          but I had writer's block.
                    (MORE)

                    CANDY (V.O.) (CONT'D)
          And since I found that piece of the
          old draft in the trash, I began
          exploring more about Candy.

INT. ROBOTECH HQ - WEEKS LATER

Charlie presents her powerpoint presentation to the staff and
interns of Robotech. She speaks to her audience while looking
at her slides on the big screen.

                    CANDY (V.O.)
          When I presented Candy to the
          company, I told them my story.
          Saying I was inspired by a
          fairytale and the meaning of the
          apple shape represents something
          creative.

YOUNG LEE CURTIS, 45, watches Charlie speaks at her
presentation. After the presentation ends, he walks up to her
and shakes her hand.

                    CANDY (V.O.)
          Everyone loved the idea, especially
          Lee Curtis, the CEO of Robotech.
          Curtis hired me after the
          presentation, and since then, I've
          been working on Candy.

END OF FLASHBACK

                    CANDY
          I never looked back at it since
          then.

INT. BEDROOM - MIDNIGHT

Billie goes to the internet and types in the search engine:
Monica Sainte. She studies Monica's social media in a
detailed manner.

Monica's social media contains tons of news headlines about
herself from her alma mater's website, her business profiles,
Monica's alma mater, and her accomplishments on the
internet.

In one of Monica's social media photos, there's an album
called "Robotech Internship Program 2006." All of the photos
in the album illustrates Monica's selfies at Robotech and
happy hour photos of Monica, Charlie, and the rest of the
interns at Alfred's Bar.

One person is tagged on the group photo, named Frankie
Hollin. Billie clicks on Frankie's name and messages her.

                    BILLIE (O.S.)
          Thanks for coming.

                    FRANKIE (O.S.)
          Always wanted to meet Charlie's
          siblings. I'm so sorry for your
          loss.

                    BILLIE (O.S.)
          Thanks, I appreciate it. Were you
          Charlie's friend?

INT. PARK - DAY

Billie and FRANKIE, 35-year-old businesswoman, both remain
across each other.

                    FRANKIE
          Well, to be honest, I wasn't close
          with Charlie, but we were great
          acquaintances. I admired her
          personality and her concept. I was
          close with Monica Sainte.

                    BILLIE
          Ah, okay. Did Charlie and Monica
          get along well?

                    FRANKIE
          Uh, I would say they were being
          close before the presentation.

                    BILLIE
          What happened at the presentation?

                    FRANKIE
          I remembered hearing a cry at the
          bathroom stall and saw Monica
          crying there. I tried to comfort
          her, but she couldn't stop crying.
          She was murmuring some words. It
          was something along the lines of
          "stupid, stupid bitch!"

                    BILLIE
          What did Charlie do?

                    FRANKIE
          Charlie didn't do anything. All she
          did was present her smart home,
          Candy. Which I thought was an
          excellent idea for Robotech.

Billie nods.

INT. LIVING ROOM - NIGHT

Billie reaches her laptop on the table and looks at more
photos of Monica's Robotech internship album, searching for
Monica's presentation. With no luck, Billie goes to all of
Monica's albums and finds an album called "Apple Project."
When Billie moves her mouse and clicks on the album…

Billie's is horrified. She sees the truth about Candy's
original developer.

Monica captures Candy's rough drafts in progress, PowerPoint
slides, and a throwback photo of young Monica dressing up as
a fairytale princess holding an apple.

Billie looks for Charlie's internship binder and sees the
exact replica of Monica's old draft of Candy by holding the
paper side by side on Billie's laptop screen.

                    BILLIE
          CANDY! What the hell is this?!

Billie shows her laptop to Candy.

                    CANDY
               WHAT?!

                    BILLIE
          Did you realize what you have
          done?

FLASHBACK

Charlie grabs a piece of paper from the trash bin and she
sees Candy's rough draft drawing.

FLASHBACK END

                    CANDY
          No, I didn't know it was hers, I
          swear!

                    BILLIE
          She didn't tell you anything about
          Candy?

                    CANDY
She did create something out of her
favorite fairytale story, but she
didn't say much. She was so
secretive.

                    BILLIE
Yeah, that explains it. Maybe
that's why you two were distant
from each other. Have you ever
wondered why Monica was quiet
around you? I mean, you two were
close.

                    CANDY
No, it never occurred to me. I
mean, we were keeping things
professional.

                    BILLIE
Have you ever got the time to talk
to Monica about the past?

                    CANDY
No…?

                    BILLIE
You guys could have talked things
out. Then maybe you wouldn't be
dead!

                    CANDY
WHAT?!

Candy electrifies Billie's apartment and turns on the TV.
Monica speaks.

                    JESSIE
          (On TV)
Now, do you have any new projects
coming up?

                    MONICA
          (On TV)
We do. As a matter of fact, let me
show you a sneak peek on one of our
latest designs.

                    JESSIE
          (On TV)
Okay, let's pop up that screen.

A photo fades in the TV screen, showing a pair of micro earpieces in various colors with the caption, "your new A.I. best friend."

                    JESSIE (CONT'D)
              (On TV)
          Wow, amazing! Are you planning to
          create Candy 2.0?

                    MONICA
          We decided to discontinued creating
          Candy. We want to honor Charlie and
          build her legacy by presenting some
          of her earliest works into
          Robotech. I thought Charlie's
          earpiece invention was great and
          she was very passionate about it.

EXT. ROBOTECH HQ - MIDNIGHT

Billie, in disguise, walks around the streets with her backpack. Then, she opens the doors of the building and heads inside.

                    BILLIE (V.O.)
          So what's the plan?

                    CANDY (V.O.)
          Go to the HQ building.

INT. ROBOTECH HQ - MIDNIGHT

The security guard lets her through when she pulls out a fake Robotech ID card. She walks towards the elevator and pushes the up button. The elevator opens, and Billie steps inside.

INT. ELEVATOR - MIDNIGHT

The elevator door opens.

                    CANDY (V.O.)
          On the 13th floor, type in the code
          4311# when you enter the office.

INT. HALLWAY - MIDNIGHT

Billie walks through the hall and sees the Robotech doors. Billie enters the number 4311# on the keypad, and the door buzzes her in.

Billie opens the door and enters the office.

                    CANDY (V.O.)
          Once you're in the office, three
          doors down to your left is our
          operations office, where the main
          membrane is. At the operations room
          type in 3323.

INT. ROBOTECH OFFICE - MIDNIGHT

Billie walks through the clean office and stares at the
coding numbers and letters spreading across the ceiling as if
she was on Wall Street.

                    BILLIE (V.O.)
          What if someone sees me?

                    CANDY (V.O.)
          They won't it's empty, but the
          office is open 24/7 for the
          employees.

Billie continues walking until she finds the operations
room.

Billie types in 3323. The door unlocks itself, and Billie
slowly opens it and sees all the robust neon red, yellow, and
green lights fading in and out of the LED light system on the
ceiling. Screens pop up of continuous coding writing across
the walls.

Billie places Candy down near the wired membrane until…

Monica enters the room. Candy remains in Billie's hands.

                    MONICA
          Oh, hello.

                    BILLIE
          Hi.

                    MONICA
          What are you doing here?

                    BILLIE
          Um, my friend who works here was
          trying to help me with my smart
          home. They're in the bathroom now,
          but they'll be back.

Monica nods.

                    BILLIE (CONT'D)
          You see, I'm having trouble with my
          Candy. She suddenly stopped
          working, and her battery died. I
          didn't know who to ask.

                    MONICA
          Okay, you could always call the
          care support.

                    BILLIE
          I know, but I don't own a computer
          and my stupid dog destroyed my
          manual.

                    MONICA
          Let me see what I can do. Can I
          have Candy?

Billie hands Candy to Monica. Monica stares at Candy.

                    BILLIE
          I saw you on the news tonight.

                    MONICA
          Oh really? Are you excited for our
          new product?

                    BILLIE
          You're discontinuing Candy because
          Charlie stole your idea, wasn't
          it?

Monica pause and looks up at Billie.

Monica throws Candy to the wall. The stainless steel smart
home remains in good condition. Not a stretch.

                    MONICA
          I'm sick and tired of Candy! Do you
          have any idea how long this
          creation took me? 15 years! It was
          my original idea! Not hers!

                    CANDY
          Monica!

Monica flinches and sees Candy, and she realizes a familiar
voice.

                    MONICA
          Charlie?

                    CANDY
          Why didn't you tell me you were
          hurt with my PowerPoint
          presentation?

FLASHBACK

INT. ROBOTECH HQ - DAY

YOUNG MONICA, 21, at her desk, draws the apple-shaped smart
home and typing in the system coding of Candy.

                    MONICA (V.O.)
          When I was young, my mother would
          read me fairytale stories. One
          story was about being poisoned by
          an apple. Instead of the apple
          being the villain, why not create
          something good out of it?

Monica piles some of her Candy drafts with the company's old
documents and shoves them in the trash bin.

                    MONICA (V.O.)
          I was swamped with my internship
          work, so I've been multitasking and
          accidentally threw my old drafts of
          Candy into the trash without
          realizing it.

Charlie picks up the trash and exists.

INT. ROBOTECH HQ OFFICE - DAY

Charle presents her PowerPoint presentation.

                    MONICA (V.O.)
          When Charlie presented her
          presentation on our final day at
          Robotech, I was shocked.

Monica looks at her Powerpoint notes and stares at Charlie's
PowerPoint screen.

At the end of Charlie's presentation, everyone clapped and
cheered. Monica, with tears in her eyes, claps. She sees
YOUNG MR. LEE CURTIS, 45, walking towards Charlie and shakes
her hand. Monica rushes to the door and leaves.

                    MONICA (V.O.)
          Mr. Curtis loved Charlie's
          presentation and offered her a
          job. My dream job. The Head Design
          of Robotech.

INT. BATHROOM - DAY

Monica screams and rips apart her notes and throws them in
the trash.

She quickly goes to one of the empty stalls and cries loudly,
using the toilet paper as her tissue.

YOUNG FRANKIE, 21, enters the bathroom and sees Monica
crying. She hugs her by calming her down.

                    FRANKIE
          Hey, it's okay.

                    MONICA (V.O.)
          I destroyed all the evidence of my
          project. Let's face it, no one
          wants a fight. So I can't be called
          Miss Plagiarize.

FLASHBACK ENDS

INT. ROBOTECH HQ - MIDNIGHT

Monica stares at Candy and Billie.

                    BILLIE
          I'm sorry to hear about all of
          this. We'll leave, don't worry.

Billie picks up Candy and take her backpack. They both headed
to the door until Monica stabs Candy with her knife. Billie
widens her eyes and cries while starring at Monica. Candy
looks at Monica.

FLASHBACK

INT. ALFRED'S BAR - NIGHT

Charlie heads to the bathroom. Monica orders two appletinis.
Once the drinks arrived, she looked both ways and sprinkled
sodium nitrate on Charlie's drink.

Charlie drinks her appletini at the dance floor and starts
feeling ill.

FLASHBACK ENDS

INT. ROBOTECH HQ - MIDNIGHT

Billie sees Monica getting close to her personal space and
quickly attacks Billie.

Both Billie and Monica fight each other off as Candy uses her
power to break free from the knife, and the knife flies to
the wall where Monica is leaning against, but the blade
missed Monica.

As soon as Billie grabs the knife on the wall, Monica slices
Billie's left arm.

Billie screams and collapses as she violently breaks her
knees. Billie holds onto her left arm.

Monica takes Candy which electrifies her hand. Monica screams
and drops Candy on the floor.

While Candy rolls away, Monica chases her with the knife.
Candy is trapped on the corner at the end of the development
room.

Monica grabs Candy again and twists the knife; Candy
screams.

Billie sneak attacks Monica from behind and pushes Monica on
the floor. The two fight, and suddenly Billie thought of an
idea.

                    CHARLIE (V.O.)
          Candy is filled with all metal and
          wires in the machine.

Billie grabs Candy and forces it into Monica's mouth. Monica
struggles to push Billie but fails as her teeth touches
Candy. Billie shoves Candy into Monica's teeth, hard. Monica
takes a bite and swallows.

Billie stands up and gets out of the way.

Monica turns her head and spits out Candy leaving a bloody
bite mark. Inside of Candy contains three colorful wires with
one broken wire in the middle.

Monica's body suddenly shakes, and she is paralyzed.

She screams as she starts choking. Her veins pops up from her
chest, as it crawls on her skin to her chin.

Her body lifts up slowly and smashes to the floor. Monica's blood rises up from her mouth like a waterfall. Monica closes her eyes.

Charlie's spirit rises up from Candy as she is transforms herself into a ghost-like figure. She gazes at the crime scene. Billie sees Charlie's ghost.

                    CHARLIE
          Thank you.

Charlie sees Monica's dead body. Closely she notices Monica wearing the Heart of Damballa necklace on her neck.

FLASHBACK

EXT. ASTORIA STREET MARKET - DAY

Charlie looks at the Heart of Damballa necklace. Monica walks to Charlie.

                    MONICA
          Oh, that does look pretty.
               (To Seller)
          If you have another one, I'll take
          one as well.

                    SELLER
          Certainly.

The seller takes an extra Heart of Damballa necklace and hands it to Monica.

FLASHBACK ENDS

INT. LIVING ROOM - ONE YEAR LATER

The MOTHER, a 45-year-old woman, brings in a package from Robotech. She opens the package which contains Candy and brings the smart home outside of her backyard.

EXT. BACKYARD - DAY

Candy is placed on the party table. Surrounded with junk food around her.

                    MOM
          Hey Candy?

Candy lights up.

                         MOM (CONT'D)
                  Play some party music.

Candy plays party music from her speakers. A fly buzzing
around Candy and lands on the smart home. Then suddenly, she
zaps the fly. The buzzing stops, and the fly falls down on
the table.

                                             FADE OUT.

                              END